SUPERHERO BUNNY LEAGUE
SAVES THE WORLD!

PAGE

D1386563

AND

SUPERHERO BUNNY LEAGUE
IN SPACE!

PAGE 33

WRITTEN AND ILLUSTRATED BY
JAMIE SMART

OXFORD
UNIVERSITY PRESS

Helping your child to read

Before they start

- Flick through the book together. Does your child like reading comic-style stories? What kinds of adventures do they think the Superhero Bunny League will have?

- Look at the front cover. Does your child think the Superhero Bunny League will be like any other superheroes they know about? Why, or why not?

During reading

- Let your child read at their own pace – don't worry if it's slow. They could read silently, or read to you out loud.

- Help them to work out words they don't know by saying each sound out loud and then blending them to say the word, e.g. *c-r-e-a-ti-o-n, creation.*

- If your child still struggles with a word, just tell them the word and move on.

- Give them lots of praise for good reading!

After reading

- Look at page 63 for some fun activities.

SUPERHERO BUNNY LEAGUE
SAVES THE WORLD!

The most brilliant scientist in the world!

Moo ha ha! I am Doctor Fuzzleglove!

And I'm about to make my most amazing creation yet …

A toasted cheese sandwich!

CLUNK!

BUNNY-CHANGING LASER ON

Oops! Wrong machine. Where's the sandwich toaster?

4

The next morning ...

Yawn!

STUMPY

Well, it's morning again.

I'm all ready for another boring day of being a rabbit.

Hang on, I can speak!

That's new!

B-b-b-b!

Blah! Blahhh!

People of Earth! I have taken over your televisions to give you an important message!

I have given all your bunny rabbits SUPER POWERS!

Erm ... accidentally.

Super powers?

How exciting! I wonder what my super powers are!

WHOOSH!

Maybe I can FLY, like that bunny!

Or lift heavy things, like that bunny!

Pfft! As if!

Or ...

Or ...

10

People of Earth!

Me again.

Huh?

Give me all your bunnies! I want the bunnies to work for ME!

All I have are silly robots.

Sorry, robots.

But SUPERBUNNIES?

Together, we could make chaos!

Moo ha ha!

I don't think so, Doctor Fuzzy-head!

Argh! Get off! Get off!

And you look ridiculous in that outfit!

I don't!

You do!

Whatever! I don't need you guys anyway.

Huff!

Ha ha!

I'll be a superhero on my OWN!

Sigh!

Hello. You look like a lonely little bunny.

?

My name is Doctor Fuzzle ...

um ...

BETTY! My name is BETTY!

Betty, all the other bunnies are special but I'm not.

SLAP!

Nonsense! Everyone's special!

Here, have a pat on the back.

Feel better?

Um ...

Good!

Bye then!

Moo ha ha!

Betty's right, I AM special somehow.

I just need to find out how.

OK, here's a big empty field where no one can see me or laugh at me.

Now let's see ...

Maybe I'm SUPER FAST?

Puff!

Wheeze!

Nope!

Maybe I'm SUPER INTELLIGENT!

Wait, what was I thinking about?

Welcome to Bunny HQ!

Where all the superbunnies live.

Superbunnies like YOU!

19

Are you the new superbunnies?

I ...

uh ...

Well, I'm Annabel, the chief science officer here at Bunny HQ.

You're ... beautiful!

Ignore him, Annabel. I'M the bunny you want. They call me HANDSOME STEVE.

Ah! New bunnies! Welcome to your new home!

HRRR!

Here at Bunny HQ, we will help you develop your super powers ...

He doesn't have any! Ha ha!

But Doctor Fuzzleglove's laser affected us ALL!

I, um. I ...

Did I hear my name?

Gasp!

BUNNY-O-VISION

I am VERY angry with you bunnies.

Come out of there and be MY superbunnies!

Or I will set my ROBOTS upon you all! Moo ha ha!

BZZ!

BZZ!

Oi! Get away from my prize-winning carrot.

BUNNY HQ

SHUSH! I'm talking to the superbunnies.

I don't understand, how did you find our secret HQ?

The tracker ...

... which I planted on Stumpy's back!

Uh oh.

BOOP! BOOP! BOOP!

Above ground …

They're taking their time.

BUNNY

SPLOOSH!

Whee!

My robots! Don't get them wet!

·:·BZZ!·:·

·:·BZZ!·:·

WHOOSH!

BZZ!

Whee!

Electricity and liquids don't mix!

SPLOSH!

Now it's your turn, Doctor!

Eek! Not likely!

Well, I need to work on my landing!

You're a hero!

A ... hero?

Three cheers for Stumpy!

Hip ... hip ... HOORAY!

Hip ... hip ... HOORAY!

Hop ... hop ... HOORAY!

Sorry I was such a bully, dude. Can I join your team?

My ... team?

Indeed! Since you four all work so well together ...

Stumpy, you will lead the ...

SUPERHERO BUNNY LEAGUE IN SPACE!

I'm Tina Tibbles for TV News, in front of a huge parade for our city's newest heroes.

BUNNIES!

Hooray!

The **SUPERHERO BUNNY LEAGUE!**

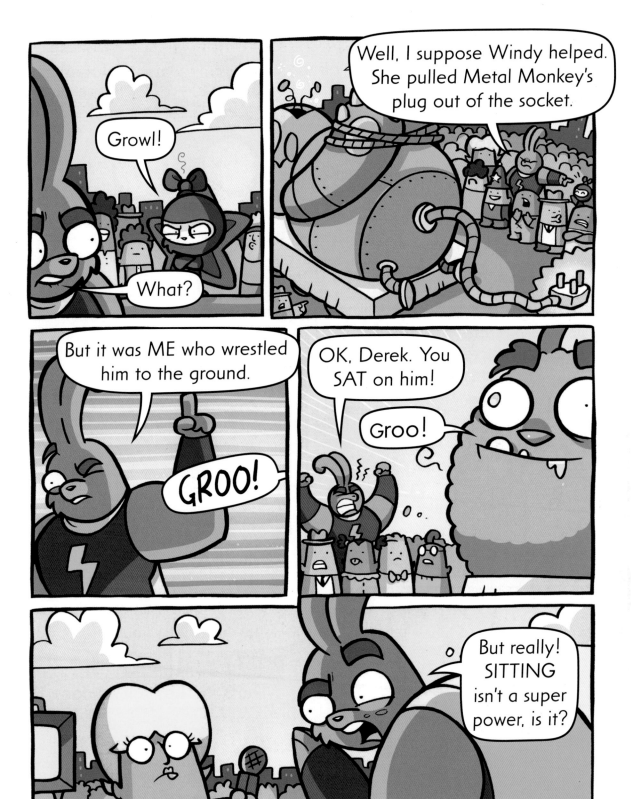

The important thing is that we worked as a team!

Together!

You have carrot in your teeth on live television!

Oh, how embarrassing!

Ha ha!

SPLOOSH!

When Stumpy gets embarrassed, he turns into liquid.

That's it! That's all he does.

Sigh!

Where's Derek?

Arr! Maybe the next planet will give us their treats!

Um, Captain?

We've caught ourselves a whopper!

Mmf!

He must have been after our cakes.

He's slowing us down!

Let's take him back!

No, let's keep him. We need a great big beast like that on our crew!

People will THROW their food at us!

44

45

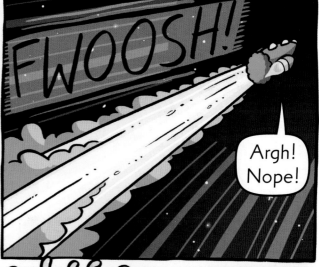

47

OK, so it's up to ME!

I'm getting the hang of it!

FWOOSH!

I'm leading my team to victory!

Oh no!

SPLAT!

I hit them with custard, Captain!

Arr! Everything's better with custard!

It's tricky to eat with our hands tied.

Exactly! You have to watch ME eating! How mean!

SLAM!

Chomp! Chomp! Chomp!

Oh.

Captain Jellybeard, we came to get our friend Derek back!

Derek? There's no Derek here.

Keep quiet, Derek! They have no idea we're hiding you out here!

53

How's it going, Windy?

Whisper!

I can hear you, you know. I have super-hearing!

You're telling him we're going to cut him loose? Why?

You'll make him angry.

Then he'll grow HUGE!

Oh, I see your plan.

FWOOP!

Groo!

Even the carrot cakes?

NO! We need to SHRINK Derek, then!

Quickly! Someone calm him down!

SCREAM!

Uh oh. Everything's going wrong and I'm tied up in a locked room!

Alone! With no one to embarrass me! This means I can't use my SUPER POWER to get out of these ropes!

You beat us this time, Superhero Bunny League.

But only because you worked together. You used your different powers to become a TEAM!

Now WE are going to work together, too! We will become a MUCH BETTER crew of dessert-stealing pirates!

WOOSH!

Hang on! You can't do that!

Ah well, Captain Jellybeard is right. We DO work well as a team after all!

Yeah! Let's go and celebrate! Carrot cake for everyone!

I'm sure we've forgotten something.

Nah ...

END!

After reading activities

Quick quiz

See how fast you can answer these questions! Look back at the stories if you can't remember.

1) In *Superhero Bunny League Saves the World!*, what makes Derek grow huge?

2) What is Bunny HQ disguised as?

3) What nickname does Handsome Steve have for Doctor Fuzzleglove?

4) In *Superhero Bunny League in Space!*, why does Captain Jellybeard come to Earth?

5) Why do Stumpy, Steve and Windy go into space?

6) How does Captain Jellybeard think the Superhero Bunnies managed to defeat him?

Try this!

- Invent your own animal superhero character! It could be based on your pet, or another animal you like.

- Draw a picture of your animal superhero. Give them a speech bubble. You could even write your own cartoon adventure about them!

Answer: 1) being angry; 2) a massive carrot; 3) Doctor Fuzzy-head; 4) to steal sweet treats and cakes; 5) to save Derek; 6) by working as a team.

OXFORD
UNIVERSITY PRESS

Great Clarendon Street, Oxford, OX2 6DP, United Kingdom

Oxford University Press is a department of the University
of Oxford. It furthers the University's objective of excellence
in research, scholarship, and education by publishing
worldwide. Oxford is a registered trade mark of Oxford
University Press in the UK and in certain other countries

Text and illustrations © Jamie Smart 2015

The moral rights of the author have been asserted

First published 2015
This edition published 2019

British Library Cataloguing in Publication Data
Data available

ISBN: 978-0-19-276975-6

10 9 8 7 6 5 4 3 2 1

Paper used in the production of this book is a natural, recyclable product
made from wood grown in sustainable forests. The manufacturing process
conforms to the environmental regulations of the country of origin.

Printed in China

Acknowledgements
Series Advisor: Nikki Gamble